William Herman T. Dau

Justificationan Essay

Read Before Augustana E. L. Conference

William Herman T. Dau

Justificationan Essay
Read Before Augustana E. L. Conference

ISBN/EAN: 9783337386856

Printed in Europe, USA, Canada, Australia, Japan

Cover: Foto ©Andreas Hilbeck / pixelio.de

More available books at **www.hansebooks.com**

Justification.

An Essay read before

AUGUSTANA E. L. CONFERENCE

AND PUBLISHED BY ITS ORDER.

———o———

The entire proceeds from sale of this pamphlet shall be devoted tc
Beneficiary Education at Concordia College, Conover, N. C.

———o———

AMERICAN LUTHERAN PUBLICATION BOARD, CHICAGO, ILL.

1894.

JUSTIFICATION.

An Essay read before Augustana E. L. Conference.

The subject which Augustana Conference has chosen to mark the beginning of its existence represents the cradle, the home, and the impregnable stronghold of the Church of the Reformation. The day on which Luther discovered the meaning of the term "the righteousness of God" is the birthday of the Lutheran Church. Upon the doctrine of "justification by grace through faith" this great church which we call our own has been reared. We do not feel at home except where we have this doctrine proclaimed; and the fortunes of this doctrine must decide the fortunes of our Church: while it stands our Church will stand, and should it ever fall, we should surrender to its assailants and confess that we have no longer any mission of really vital importance to men to perform.

In what glowing terms the Confessions of our Church speak of this doctrine! "This article concerning justification by faith is, as the Apology declares, the leading article of the whole christian doctrine; without which a disturbed conscience can have no sure consolation, or rightly conceive the riches of the grace of Christ; as Dr. Luther has written: If this single article remain pure, the whole christian community will also remain pure and harmonious, and without any factious; but if it remain not pure, it is impossible to resist any error or fanatical spirit." (Form. of Conc. Decl. III, 630*) Thy Apology calls it "the principal and most important article of the whole christian doctrine," and says: "It contributes especially to a clear, correct apprehension of the Holy Scriptures;" "it alone shows the way to the unspeakable treasure and the true knowledge of Christ;" "yea, it is the only key to the whole Bible." (Apol. III, 156.) Regarding this article Dr. Luther professes: "In my heart dwelleth alone, and shall there dwell, this only article, to wit, faith in my dear Lord Christ, which is the sole beginning, middle, and end of all my spiritual and divine thoughts, which I happen to entertain, at any time, whether by day or by night." (Walch, VIII, 1524.)

It is worth while to hear Luther discourse on the great find which he, the miner's son, was led to make in the year 1519, when digging deep in the gold-mines of God's Word. He tells

---

*) Quotations from Book of Concord according to Second New Market Edit.

the story thus: "I had, in truth, a cordial desire and longing correctly to understand St. Paul's Epistle to the Romans, and, so far, nothing had prevented me, save only that one little word "justitia Dei"' (the righteousness of God) in the 17. verse of the first chapter, where Paul says, the righteousness of God is revealed in the gospel. I intensely hated this word "the righteousness of God," and, as was the custom and practice of all teachers, I had not been taught and instructed otherwise than that I must understand it as the philosophers do, namely that it denoted that righteousness by which God is righteous in Himself, performs righteous acts, and punishes all sinners and un-righteous persons, which righteousness is called essential (formalis) or active (activa). Now, my condition was this: although I was leading the life of an holy and unblameable monk, yet I found myself a great sinner before God, and also of an anxious and disquieted conscience, having no confidence in my ability to reconcile God by my works of atonement and merits. Thus, I did not at all love this righteous and angry God who punishes sinners, but hated Him, and, (if this was no blasphemy or should be regarded as such) secretly I was angry with God in good earnest; frequently I would say: Is God not satisfied with heaping upon us poor, miserable sinners who, by virtue of original sin, have already been condemned to eternal death, all manner of misery and sorrow in this life, besides the terror and threats of the law, and must he still increase this misery and heart-ache by the gospel, and by its voice and proclamation menace us still further and make known his righteousness and serious wrath? Here I oftentimes could wax hot in my confused conscience; still I continued my meditations on dear St. Paul, to ascertain what he would possible mean at this place, and I felt a hearty craving and desire to know it. With such thoughts I spent days and nights until, by the grace of God, I perceived the connection of the words, namely in this wise: The righteousness of God is revealed in the gospel: as it is written, The just shall live by faith. Thence I have learnt to understand that righteousness of God in which the righteous through the grace and gift of God live by faith alone, and I perceived this to be the meaning of the apostle, that by the gospel is revealed the righteousness which is valid before God, in which God from grace and pure mercy justifies us, which, in Latin, is called justitia passiva (passive righteousness) as it is written: The just shall live by his faith. Presently I felt that I had been entirely born anew and that I had right here found a door wide open and leading straightway into paradise; moreover, now the dear Scriptures looked at me quite different from what they had before; accordingly, I hurriedly ran through the whole Bible, prying into as many passages as I could remember, and, according to this same rule, I collected all its interpretations also with regard to other terms; e. g., that God's work means this, that God Himself works in us; God's power, that by which He makes us mighty and strong; God's wisdom, that by which he makes us wise; also other terms: the strength of God, the salvation of God, the glory of God, etc. Now, as much as I had before hated this term "the righteousness of God" in good earnest, as highly I now began to prize and esteem it, considering it the word dearest and most comforting to me, and this self-same place in St. Paul verily became to me the true gate of paradise." (Halle XIV, 460 ff.) A brief account shall now be given of this doctrine.

RANGE OF JUSTIFICATEON.

Literally translated the verb "justify" means *to make just;* justification, therefore, is the act of making just. In what sense we are *made* just will appear anon. The very signification of this word reveals the wide range of the act. It pertains to the unjust, only to these, but to these in their entirety. None are made just who are already just; "they that are whole have no need of a physician, but they that are sick: I came not to call the righteous, but sinners to repentance;" (Mark 2: 17.) "I say unto you, that likewise joy shall be in heaven, over one sinner that repenteth, more than over ninety and nine just persons, which need no repentance," (Luke 15: 7) — these words of Our Savior state the limits both of His mission on earth and of justification.

But, if justification pertains to "the ungodly," (Rom. 4: 5.) then all men are in need of it; for "all have sinned and come short of the glory of God;" (Rom. 3: 23.) "if we say that we have no sin, we deceive ourselves, and the truth is not in us." (1 John 1: 8.) The first sinner was the first subject for justification; Adam was justified; and judgment will not come upon the world until the last sinner that repents is justified.

Justification, then, deals with sinners and sin. What constitutes a sin? "Sin is the transgression of the law." (1 John 3: 4.) A man clear of all lawlessness or "anomia", as the Greek text has it, would be a rightous person; no charge could be brought against him. Such a person Adam was before the fall; he lived up to every requirement of the law of God; and as he feared no accuser then, so he needed no one to justify him. All that justification can do for a sinner, he already had: justification renders a person unimpeachable by the law; it pronounces him to be of such a character as the divine law requires in him.

JUSTIFICATION A CHANGE.

Accordingly, *justification* represents *a most wonderful change.* In Luke 18. we see "the publican standing afar off," not daring to "lift up so much as his eyes unto heaven, but smiting upon his breast, saying, God be merciful to me a sinner." (vv. 13, 14.) This moment the publican is conscious of but one thing, his guilt; he stands before the bars of divine justice and himself pleads guilty. In the next verse, however, the Savior assures us, "I tell you this man went down to his house justified." In the twinkling of an eye this sinner had, in the eyes of God, become a saint, because God had justified him. A moment ago every commandment had been against him; the whole decalogue, like ten eye- and ear-witnesses, had marched up to the bar of justice, and had there deposited their testimony; the first commandment had said, He has broken me, the second had said, He has broken me, and so on to the tenth, and the publican's head had sunk upon his breast, as his own conscience within him had confirmed the testimony of every one of these witnesses. And, in spite of this overwhelming evidence, the sinner is pronounced not guilty, i. e. God says, he has the full righteousness of the law; I find no charge against him. How is this possible? *Whence is this righteousness* which the publican could offer to the Lord, his judge?

WHENCE THE RIGHTEOUSNESS OF JUSTIFICATION?

It is evident that the righteousness which God finds in the sinner whom he justifies, cannot be the sinner's own righteousness. *It must have been borrowed* from some one else; and since no man is in possession of such righteousness as is required, it must have been borrowed from some one who is more than man. This person who is to lend his righteousness to sinners, must, indeed, be a human being, because the righteousness, which is required in justification, is such as God demands from human beings, from subjects to his law, but he must be something besides a human being, since no mere human being could acquire the righteousness that is necessary. Now, who is this person that lends, yea gives his righteousness to sinners? Ah, you know Him: He is the God-Man, Jesus Christ. "This is his name whereby he shall be called, THE LORD OUR RIGHT-EOUSNESS" — so says the prophet in the Old Testament, (Jerem. 23:6) and his compeer in the New corroborates this by saying: "Christ Jesus is made unto us righteousness." (1 Cor. 1:30.)

Twofold righteousness of Christ.

Before proceeding further, however, let us mark that we shall now speak of that righteousness which Christ possesses as God-Man, not as God. It is the former which is being imputed to the sinner in justification. By giving us His *divine* righteousness Christ would make us, not justified sinners, but gods like Himself. His divine righteousness is an attribute of His divine nature; this He shares with no man, but with the Father and the Holy Ghost; this righteousness He possesses from eternity. However, the righteousness of which we shall now speak is not a part of His divine essence; is not from eternity, but has been subsequently acquired in the fulness of time; it is this *acquired righteousness* which Christ permits all justified sinners to share with Him.

Basis of Justification; — The Savior's Work.

How was this second righteousness acquired? In order that it might truly be a man's righteousness, He who was to acquire it must, in the first place, be made a man. Such Christ became through His incarnation; in assuming our human nature, however, Christ assumed also the responsibilities and duties of our human nature. Paul says: "When the fulness of time was come, God sent forth His Son, *made of a woman*, MADE UNDER THE LAW." (Gal. 4:4.) God required of Christ all that He had, at any time, required of man, perfect fulfillment of all the ten commandments, perfect fear, love, and trust of God above all things, perfect love of his neighbor, perfect submission also to the ordinances of God in His then Church on earth. "It becometh us to fulfill all righteousness" — these are the Savior's own words. (Matth. 3:15.)

Christ, then, was like his fellowmen in every respect save one: original and actual sin. And, in this respect he needed not to become like his fellowmen; for sin is not an essential part of our human nature, but an accidental addition entailed upon man after his creation. The first man Adam, when leaving his Creator's hands, was a sinless being; such a sinless being Christ was; he was the second Adam. (Rom. 5: 14; 1 Cor. 15: 45.) True, He was exposed to all the ills, subject to all infirmities of this life, and capable of being tempted as we are; the difference, however, between Him and all other man is this: He kept His original righteousness, which the first Adam had thrown away; he began His life in accordance with the law, His daily conduct was unblameable, so much so that He could challenge the closest scrutiny of his adversaries and say: "Which of you convinceth me of sin?" (John 8: 46) and He finished His earthly career as He had begun it, so that the writer to the Hebrews can say of Him that He "is holy, harmless, undefiled, seperate from sinners." (Hebr. 7: 26.) Yea, it is really as the same writer says: "We have not an high priest which cannot be touched with the feeling of our infirmities; but was in all points tempted like as we are, yet without sin." (Heb. 4: 15.)

What was the purpose of God in sending His Son to acquire perfect righteousness by what is called, *His active obedience?* For His own person the Son needed no such righteousness, as He was already righteous by reason of His divine nature. Should it be necessary for God to acquire the righteousness of the law, it must be argued that also the Father and the Holy Ghost should have become incarnate and fulfilled the law. Or was it God's aim to prove to the whole world, by the example of the man Christ, that such a life as His was possible, had once been possible for our ancestor Adam, and that, hence, their sin was an inexcusable error and their condemnation just? Alas! that needed no proof, God's Word and man's conscience sufficiently arguing that point. No, this was the reason: "As by the offence of one judgment came upon all men to condemnation; even so by the righteousness of one the free gift came upon all men unto justification. For as by one man's disobedience many were made sinners, so by the obedience of one shall many be made righteous." (Rom. 5: 18, 19.) This is the divine answer to the question: To what end did Christ fulfill the law? He did so in order that there might be a righteousness such as was required of man, which should be counted to man as his own in the place of the one which man had lost and could not regain.

In God's eyes, therefore, the life of Christ was not simply the life of this one person born of the Virgin Mary, it was not simply the life of one individual out of the millions which people the earth, but it was virtually the life of the whole human race in this One Man. God viewed His Son as standing in the place of all men; whatever His Son accomplished God regarded as having been accomplished by all men; and as He must concede perfect righteousness to His Son, so He concedes perfect righteousness to all men in His Son. The Father has made the Son a general representative, a substitute, a vicar, a proxy of all men, and when He pronounces His Son just and holy, he so pronounces all men, when He raises His Son to the state of glory, He raises all men thither. *In Christ God has, once and for all times, justified all men.* And in order that all men may know this He has had a true account of the vicarious work of His Son written by inspired men, He has instituted the office of the holy ministry and has commissioned its incumbents with authority to make this announcement in His name: "Christ is the end of the law for righteousness to every one that believeth;" (Rom. 10: 4.) i. e. God has made this known to all men: You are already righteous and should only claim your righteousness in my beloved Son. Look not to the law; look to Christ! The law is in Him; He has fulfilled it and proven Himself greater than the law; He is your righteousness, because I have counted you as being in Him, and require of you nothing. This believe!

Accordingly, the righteousness which the sinner obtains in justification is Christ's, or, in other words, man is justified in view of the perfect obedience of Christ, which is declared to be his own he having claimed it as his own by faith.

The Expiation.

But is this all that man receives in his justification? No, this is only one half. To use a simile, there are, in God's accounts, two pages to every man's name; on one page are entered all man's defiencies, what he has neglected to do, his sins of omission. This page is cancelled in view of the obedience of Christ, God substituting in its place all Christ's merits. On the other page are entered all man's iniquities, offences, what he has done, his sins of commission. Something must be done with regard to *them* before the sinner can be pronounced free. Men may say: Let-by-gones be by-gones! not so God, who has said: "The soul that sinneth, it shall die", (Ezek. 18: 20) and whose "words are yea in Him and Amen in Him." (2 Cor. 1: 20) Provided, therefore, this page be blottet out, the entire right-

ousness of Christ will be of no benefit to the sinner; he should
have to die nevertheless. Now, Paul tells us, that Christ has
"blotted out the handwriting of ordinances that was against
us, which was contrary to us, and took it out of the way, nailing
it to his cross." (Col. 2:14.)

Yes, think of the cross. Why did Jesus die? Death had
been announced to Adam as the wages of his sin, and Christ was
without sin. His death cannot be accounted for in any other
way than in that in which we accounted for his incarnation and
fulfillment of the law: it was representative and vicarious. God
counted to Christ not only the responsibilities and duties of
mankind but also their crimes. God incriminated Christ for
humanity.

Throughout the Scriptures Christ stands before us not only
as the Immaculate and Holy One, but also as the great sinner.
"The Lord hath laid on him the iniquity of us all." (Isa. 53:6.)
He, "his own self bore our sins in his own body on the tree,"
(1 Pet. 2:24.) so both the prophet and the apostle inform us.
Yea, Paul puts it even stronger when he says, "God hath made
him to be sin for us;" likewise, "Christ hath redeemed us
from the curse of the law being made a curse for us." (2 Cor.
5:21; Gal. 3:13.) He does say "a sinner," "a cursed man,"
but uses abstract terms to signify sin in the aggregate, all curses
in a heap, so that they seem as one object.

And, as to the vicarious signification of the suffering and
death of Our Lord, it is impossible to conceive of a clearer
statement than that made by the evangelist of the Old Testament, Isaiah, who says: "Surely, *he* hath borne *our* griefs, and
carried *our* sorrows: yet *we* did esteem *him* stricken, smitten of
God, and afflicted. But *he* was wounded for *our* transgressions,
he was bruised for *our* iniquities: the chastisement of *our* peace
was upon *him;* and with *his* stripes *we* are healed." (Isa. 53:4,
5.) The representative character of Christ's doing and dying
is one of the banner truths of the Word, voiced with clarion
distinctness in both Testaments. Peter says: "Christ also hath
once suffered for sins, the just for the unjust, (1 Pet. 3:18.)
"for", i. e., in the place of. Paul says: "When we were yet
without strength in due time Christ died for the ungodly. For
scarcely for a righteous man will one die: yet peradventure for
a good man some would even dare to die. But God commendeth
his love toward us, in that, while we were yet sinners, Christ
died for us;" (Rom. 5:6-8.) "for", i. e., in the place of. Cai-

aphas, the blind priest, like Balaam's ass, spoke God's will, when, advocating the removal of the Lord, he said in the council of the Pharisees: "It is expedient for us, that one man should die for the people and the whole nation perish not." (John 11: 51.)

The guilt of mankind having been transferred to the Son of God, it follows, that, in the sight of God, there is no longer any guilt resting on mankind. The emperor Napoleon would not permit the second enlistment of a man who had sent a substitute for himself to his country's defense, which substitute had been killed in battle; the emperor decided that the principal had died in his alternate, that, in the eyes of his country, he had ceased to live. God is, to say the least, fully as just; God has meted out to the whole world the full reward of their iniquities, when He hurled His only Begotten into the throes of temporal and eternal death. It is a divine, not a human, principle of retribution, that no malefactor shall be punished twice for the same offense. In the agonies of the Man of Sorrows upon the cursed tree the deeds of violence and unrighteousness of all sinners are punished, and through the moans and tears of that awful day on which the Prince of Glory died we hear the voice of God making this announcement to an awe-struck universe: Herewith I draw the pencil through the page of your guilt; you are "redeemed from the curse of the law;" (Gal. 3: 13.) "you are saved from wrath through him;" (Rom. 5: 9.) "he has made peace through the blood of his cross." (Col. 1: 20.)

The incrimination of Christ, then, is the exculpation of the sinner; with the same decree which imposes the sinner's penalty upon Christ, the real criminal is delivered. And this freedom from the curse of the law is imparted to the sinner in justification. In view of the death of Christ God checks his own arm which is about to deal the sinner the avenging blow, and says: You shall live by your faith.

The Book of Concord calls attention to an error of certain theologians who had divided Christ into Christ, the God, and Christ, the Man; it says: "We believe, teach, and confess unaminously, that Christ is our righteousness, neither according to the divine nature alone, nor yet according to the human nature alone, but *the whole Christ* according to both natures, in or through that obedience alone which he as God and man, rendered to the Father even unto death, and by which he has merited for us forgiveness of sins and eternal life; as it is written Rom. 5: 19:

'For as by one man's disobedience many were made sinners, so by the obedience of one shall many be made righteous.'" (F. C. Epit. III, 560.)

Meaning of the term justify.

Having seen what it is that the sinner receives in justification we may now return to the word 'justify', which means to make just, for the purpose of ascertaining in what sense the justified are *made* just. Justification, in no wise, affects the substance of man, but only his moral relation to God. As to his substance man remains in and after justification what he was before justification: a sinner. His sins are not materially removed from him or out of him, so that after justification he should be altogether without any sin. Nor is a new substance added to or infused into him by his justification. This would be against the actual experience of certain justified sinner's of whom the divine records tell us; e. g.: we hear the justified Paul exclaim: "O wretched man that I am! who shall deliver me from the body of this death?" (Rom. 7:24.) The same Paul writes to the justified Galatians: "The flesh lusteth against the Spirit, and the Spirit against the flesh: and these are contrary the one to the other: so that ye cannot do the things that ye would." (Gal. 5:17.) Nor should passages like these be interpreted as meaning that the apostle, in them, complains' of *occasional* infirmities which have *not yet* been removed by justification; for, that would make justification a continuous act rising in degrees from incipiency to perfection; a view which is not only unscriptural but also robs justification of all comfort. Paul says: "We shall be made the righteousness of God in him," (1 Cor. 5:21.) The peculiar language of this text is of decisive importance; the apostle does not say: We shall be made righteous; but, We shall be made righteousness; he does not use an adjective, but a noun. Now, an adjective or quality-word admits of degrees; a righteous person can become more righteous and most righteous. But a noun or object-word always represents one whole integral thing, unless it occurs in connection with a term of measure, which is not the case in this passage. The apostle does not say: we shall be made some righteousness, but *the righteousness*. Hence, in justification God counts to the sinner *all*, ALL righteousness of Christ; He does not say: I will justify to the extent of 25 degrees for the present, reserving 75 degrees for some future period, but whenever he justifies he justifies 100 per cent. —

Only imagine the condition of one being gradually justified. Suppose, he should be justified 10 degrees to-day, 7 degrees a month from now, and after two months he dies, having reached in all, say 32 degrees. "Whosoever shall keep the whole law, and yet offend in one point, he is guilty of all," (James 2:10.) — this saying will then rob him of what little justification he has. What should such a justification have booted the thief on the cross whose time of grace was already at an end when it had merely begun? Another point: how is man ever to be made certain that he has attained to the last degree of justification, granting it to be a work of continuity and gradation. No, no, no! Justification makes a person entirely wholly, completely, perfectly righteous and that in as much time as it requires to pronounce these words: Thy sins are forgiven thee!

Justification, then, is not that act by which sins are rooted out of, extirpated from the nature of man, but it is an act by which they are *declared cancelled*, stricken from the accounts, forgiven and forgotten by God. The Form of Concord says: "When, however, we teach that we are born anew and justified through the operation of the Holy Spirit, it must not be understood, as if no unrighteousness whatever adhered to the justified and regenerate, in their essence or in their conduct after regeneration, but that Christ with his perfect obedience covers all their sins which still adhere to them in this life." (Decl. III, 632.) We receive righteousness in the same manner as Christ received sins; the sins of mankind were not infused into his nature, but were only reckoned, counted, imputed to Him. The Redeemer bore about the same relation to the sins of the world, as a person bears to the coat which he wears: our sins were hung over Him like a cloak, and thus He bore them; He never actually committed one of them. In like manner the righteousness of Christ is hung over us in justification, and we wear it as "our beauty and our glorious dress;" we have not wrought out one particle of it, nor has one particle of it been wrought out *in* us by Christ. The garment of the Savior on Calvary was a borrowed one: our wedding garment is a gift of God; all the sins which Christ bore had been committed outside of his body: all the righteousness which the sinner receives in justification has been achieved outside of himself; Christ was made sin by imputation: we are made righteousness by imputation. This means that the entire act of justification is a moral act taking place in God's mind, extending to and terminating upon the sinner; in this act God says: This man is now a sinner and will remain a sinner until he is rid of his flesh and out of this world, yet I will not regard, consider, esteem him as such, because he has the righteousness of Christ. I will, in view of the same, regard, consider, esteem him as righteous.

So the *Confessions* of our Church speak of justification. In the third article of the Form of Concord which treats of justification, there are found expressions like these: "*imputing* to us the righteousness of the obedience of Christ;" (p. 560.) "*reputed as just;*" (p. 561.) "*accounted* holy and righteous;" (p. 561.) "righteousness which is *imputed* to them;" (p. 561.) "*absolved* and *declared* free;" (p. 630.) "faith is *counted unto us for* righteousness;" (p. 631.) "*account as* released;" (p. 631.) "they are *pronounced and accounted* righteous and just;" (p. 635.) The same article offers the following definition: "JUSTIFY SIGNIFIES TO DECLARE JUST and absolved from sin and to account as released." Also the following statements: "We believe, teach, and confess that ACCORDING TO THE PHRASEOLOGY OF THE HOLY SCRIPTURES THE WORD TO JUSTIFY, in this article, SIGNIFIES TO ABSOLVE, that is, TO PRONOUNCE A SENTENCE OF RELEASE FROM SIN, as illustrated in the following passages Prov. 17:15; Rom. 8:33." (p. 561.) Again: "As their (i. e. the justified person's renewal is only commenced and remains imperfect in this life, and as sin dwells in the flesh, even of the regenerate, *righteousness of faith before God consists in a gracious imputation of the righteousness of Christ*, without the addition of our works; so that our sins are forgiven, *covered over, and not imputed* to us. Rom. 4:6–8." (p. 633.)

Has the term 'justify' this meaning in the *Scriptures?* We have heard that the framers of our Confessions base their interpretation on "the phraseology of the holy Scriptures." Indeed, the Lutheran Church should not teach this meaning of the term, were it not scriptural. Bible scholars tell us that this word occurs 38 times in the New Testament, and that in every place it denotes a judicial, or forensic act of God, such an act as is that of a judge who pronounces a criminal "not guilty." Let us look at some of the passages. Luke 16:15: "And he said unto them, ye are they which justify themselves before men: but God knoweth your hearts." Now, if justify here should mean to "make just by removing sin," or by "infusing righteousness," we should not understand why the Savior chides these people; for, in that case, their action would seem highly commendable. But, what the Pharisees did was this: they declared themselves just, they pretended righteousness, while they were unrighteous; and that was a great sin. — Luke 7:29: "The publicans justified God." Now, surely it would be absurd, to say the least, to interpret this text thus: the publicans made God just, infused righteousness into God. No, it means, they pronounced Him, declared Him to be a just God. Luther rightly translates: "sie gaben Gott recht." — Moreover we find the term "justify" accompanied by its forensic correlative or opposite, "condemn"; e. g., Matth. 12:37: "By thy words thou shalt be justified, and by thy words thou shalt be condemned." It is absurd to imagine that when a judge pronounces a sentence on a criminal he fills him with condemnation or with righteousness; he simply declares the defendant guilty or not guilty. In exactly the same meaning the term is used with reference to justification, Rom. 15:16; "The judgment was by one to condemnation, but the free gift is of many offences unto justification." The judgment, i. e., the sentence. Literally rendered this verse reads: For, on the one hand, the sentence resulted in condemnation on account of one man; on the other hand the gracious gift, (gracious,) because of many offences, resulted in a justifying sentence. However, what need is there of any human interpretation of the term "justify"? Have we not the interpretation of the Holy Ghost in John 3:18 and 5:24? For, "condemn" and "come into condemnation" is the translation of Greek words which really mean "judge" and "enter into judgment."

JUSTIFICATION AND SANCTIFICATION.

The distinction between justification by imputation and justification by infusion, between *making* just, and *pronouncing* just, is of vast importance in practical life. The Lutheran Church, on account of her doctrine of justification by imputation, has been and is being charged with rejecting good works, or, at least, with not assigning to this topic the place which it deserves in the cycle of apostolic doctrines. This charge, if it has not its origin in malice, is surely begotten of ignorance. For, the framers of the Confessions of our Church have not left the world in doubt regarding our views of the necessity of good works. "Nor do we," so they say, "on the other hand, mean that we are allowed or that we should commit sins, and persevere and remain in them, without repentance, conversion, and amendment of life." (F. C. Decl. III, 632.) The true Lutheran Church has at all times championed scriptural teaching and scriptural living; true faith, and the genuine fruits thereof, good works. But she assigns to each its proper place, domain, and period. Rightly the Lutheran Church excludes from the article of justification the good works of the justified. Hear the Confessions. "If we wish to retain in its purity the article concerning justification, great diligence and care are to be observed, lest that which precedes faith, and that which follows it, be at the same time intermingled into the article concerning justification, as necessary and pertaining to it. For it is not one and the same thing to speak of conversion and of justification." (F. C. Decl. III, 633.)

In his spiritual life the christian passes through several stages. He is first a child of wrath, and made to feel the burden and terror of sin; this is contrition, the first stage of repentance. Next faith is kindled in him, and so soon as he has faith he is also justified. Immediately thereafter a third stage begins which continues until the christian's death; this third stage is called by various names, such as sanctification, conversion, (in the wide sense,) renewal, new life, new obedience. In this last stage, after justification, a christian begins to perform good works, which, indeed, never reach the perfection demanded by the law, either in quality or in quantity, but which are, nevertheless, acceptable to God because they are performed by a justified person. Accordingly, a true christian, in his lifetime, is possessor of *a twofold righteousness:* one, the righteousness of justification, which is full and perfect; the other, the righteousness of sanctification, which is never perfect, which is greater in the one, less in the other; which should continually increase, but may at any time decrease; which never becomes consummate in this life. According to the righteousness of sanctification there are degrees among christians: St. Paul, Augustine, Luther, yea, every christian is, in this sense, more righteous than I; but, according to the righteousness of justification there are no degrees; by virtue of this righteousness I am fully as righteous as St. Peter, the Mother of God, or any other living or glorified saint.

Great damage is done to the faith, life, and hope of christians by confounding these two righteousnesses. In all our dealings with God we should tightly close our eyes to the righteousness which we have by sanctification. Whenever our sins trouble us we should not attempt to counteract their force by the beggarly virtues which we may possibly be able to set against them; for, even in regenerate christians sins far outweigh virtues. We should then rivet our eyes upon the gospel which tells us of "the better righteousness than that of the Pharisees and scribes," (Matth. 5: 20.) the righteousness of Christ which we have by justification. As soon as we follow the wicked bend of our flesh, which is always inclined to self-glorification, we shall be undone; our merits will melt in the fire of the fierce anger of God, like snow before an April sun. The merits of Christ, however, have withstood the test of this fire and have gone through unscathed; they alone are reliable.

"Wherefore," so says the Form of Concord, "even if converted persons and believers have an incipient renewal, sanctification, love, virtue and good works, yet they cannot and must not be drawn into, or intermingled in the article of justification before God; so that the honor of Christ the Redeemer may remain and that, since our new obedience is imperfect and impure, *disturbed consciences may have a* SURE *consolation.*" (F. C. Decl. III, 632.)

Furthermore, a confusion of the two kinds of righteousness, instead of quickening the new life into greater activity, rather retards it. For a christian finding himself impeded in a thousand ways on his path of godliness, cannot but lose courage, if he depends on what *he* does; it is too little to satisfy his own heart, if he is upright. After a short contest he will throw up his hands, and grow indifferent, cold, dead. Confidence in the perfect righteousness, however, which we possess in Christ is an ever active incentive to new and better endeavors in holiness. A true christian knows that he is safe, though he slips and misses his aim, and finds the gnawing worm even in his best works.

The righteousness, therefore, which we have by faith, is our sole trust and stay. It is the great sheet anchor of the ship of faith in which we are sailing heavenward across the tempest-tossed sea of this life; we lower it when the mad waves threaten destruction; it sinks; it catches in the Rock of Ages; it holds with firm grasp and keeps us unmoved while the surges sweep over the main-deck, and carry off masts, rigging, and all. This righteousness is our pilgrim's fare, our manna and water, on our journey to the Canaan which is above; it is the pillow on which we finally lay our weary head, when, with the shades of death gathering about our breaking eyes, we lie down like Jacob on the barren heath of this dreary and desolate world, and go to sleep, and in blissful dreams behold visions of paradise and God's angels descending to lift us up and carry us home to the glory of the righteous, to the saints in light.

For a pure presentation of the article of justification two more points require our attention.

CAUSES OF JUSTIFICATION.

The first of these I shall state by means of this question: *What causes God to justify?* In this question should be included such a matter as this: What has urged, impelled and moved God to arrange for the work of atonement by which Christ has wrought out the righteousness that is necessary for justification and by which God has already justified the whole world in toto; and what urges, impels and moves God to confer this righteousness upon the individual sinner?

MEANING OF THE TERM "CAUSE".

It is well known that the teachers of our Church in their private dogmatical writings make a very liberal use of the term "cause"; they use it as a class-name and connect it with qualifying adjectives, and by means of such compound terms or phrases they designate every material part or point of any doctrine which they present. Thus, Baier, in his treatise on justification, enumerates the following "causes": 1. the efficient cause, the triune God; 2. the internal impelling cause, the goodness and gracious favor of God; 3. the principal external impelling or meritorious cause, the mediator Christ in respect to his active and passive obedience; 4. the less principal external impelling cause, faith in Christ. Evidently this is a very wide use of the term "cause", so wide that it sometimes puzzles us, e. g. when we read that faith is classified under the "impelling causes" of justification. We do not so use the term "cause" at the present time; whenever we speak of a "cause", we mean that power or motive, which impels or moves to something, and results in something which we call its effect; thus we say: like causes, like effects. Now, our Confessions have not adopted the phraseology of the dogmaticians; they use the term "cause" as it is commonly used, to denote an impelling, or let me say, a causing cause. Already this consideration is a sufficient reason why we should also use the term "cause" in its common, popular, every day signification; for, we are not obliged to follow the private teachings of theologians but only the public Confessions of our Church. There is, however, another reason why we should so use the term "cause", and that is this: whenever the term "cause" is, at present, used in the sense of the dogmaticians, and no explanation is given along with it, it is liable to engender error, and that sometimes of a serious nature. False doctrine may lurk behind a single term, and whenever we have reason to suspect false doctrine, we should simply take the club of the common man's mode of speaking and beat upon the bush of the learned man's phraseology to ascertain what kind of game is in hiding there. We should then inquire, in what sense the term "cause" is being used.

Two Causes.

What, then, is there that is of such inherent virtue and power as to be able to impel God, in the first place, to supply the necessary requisite for justification, the needed righteousness, and, in the second place, to confer this righteousness upon the individual sinner? Shall we look for such a cause in man? Impossible; for the entire plan of salvation was already laid down before man was; and this plan looks to justification and glorification. Nor could an angel, for this same reason, have supplied a cause which could have moved God. We, therefore look for the cause impelling God in God Himself, and here we find two causes which the apostle Paul comprehends in one statement when he writes: "Being justified freely by his grace through the redemption that is in Christ Jesus." (Rom. 3:24.) According to this statement our justification is due to the free grace of God, and the redemption of Christ.

The Grace of God, the first cause.

The grace of God is the first cause. What do we mean by "the grace of God"? The Romish sect teaches that the imparted grace, the grace of God infused into man, or, in other words, man's good works justify. For a number of reasons this is a false assumption.

1. To argue that a sinner receives grace, and, having received it, is justified by God, would mean that a sinner can be in possession of God's grace and yet not be justified. It would create a kind of intermediate estate between man's natural condition of unrighteousness and his later condition of righteousness. This is against the Scriptures which know man only as

an enemy or as a child of God, and nowhere speak of a stage of suspense and indecision.

2. If the grace of God that is in the sinner, or, in other words, the sinner's good works, justify, it follows that justification is a work of degrees and that it remains imperfect in this life. For, as has been shown before, it is impossible for a sinner to fulfill all righteousness, as long as he remains in the flesh. Hence, this grace of God could never save a sinner.

3. If the grace of God in man causes him to justify a sinner, then the sinner by means of the grace, which he had received, must also have caused God to send the Redeemer. John 3:16 should, in that case, read thus: The sinners so loved the redemption which God proposed to procure by His Son that God was moved to send His Son etc. etc.

4. The Scriptures use certain synonyms for the term "the grace of God," such as "the riches of his mercy," "his great love," (Eph. 2:4.) "the kindness and love of God." (Tit. 3:4.) These synonyms we would be justified in substituting for the term "grace", and then we should argue that "the riches of God's mercy" in man, "the love of God" in man, "God's kindness and love" in man cause him to justify the sinner. Which would mean, that God renders man merciful, kind, loving, and thereupon justifies the loving, kind, and merciful whoremonger, thief or manslayer. As a bundle of absurdities such a doctrine is without a parallel.

No, the grace of God which moves Him to justify is His everlasting, divine love; that virtue by which God is inclined to have compassion, to pity, to *be* merciful and gracious; it is God's own heart that prompts Him to justify, not the sinner's heart. Paul says, it is "the love wherewith he loved us" (Eph. 2:4) not the love wherewith we love Him. We believe an extra-human, not an intra-human justifying grace. And this grace of God which God has as God, which is one of His essential attributes, is *the* cause, the prime cause, the cause of causes, of our salvation and of everything thereunto pertaining, also of our justification. Without it, there could never have been a beginning of the mere thought of the redemption of mankind, and unless the sinner views God as the gracious God, who is "slow to anger, full of compassion, and who forgives iniquities, transgressions and sins," (Eph. 34:6, 7.) he will never even begin to know what justification means.

The Merits of Christ the second cause.

This first cause, — first in order and first in importance, — virtually includes the second cause before mentioned, the propitation of Christ by His living and dying, which is called the meritorious cause, or that in view of, on account of, for the sake of, or in consideration of which the gracious God justifies. John 3: 16, that wonderful passage which presents the whole Bible in a nutshell, teaches that the coming of Christ is a result of the love of God. The first cause has become manifested in the second; the gracious God is portrayed in the image of the suffering God. "Philip, he that hath seen me, hath seen the Father." John 14: 9. This cause must, then, be viewed and treated accordingly. It does not do away with the gratuitous favor of God in the work of our justification, nor is this favor excluded from it; not only because this second cause flows from the first, but also because it constantly appeals to the first: it is the gracious God that accepts the merits of Christ in lieu of our own.

The principal proof-text for this part of the doctrine, Rom. 3: 24, evidently has this meaning, that in the act of justifying the eyes of God are on the price of redemption which Christ has paid for sinners and that, moved and impelled by it, He forgives sin. In like manner, God is said to have "made him to be sin for us, who knew no sin," that *we* might be made the righteousness of God *in him.*" (2 Cor. 5: 21.) And here belongs what is said about Christ 1. Cor. 1: 30. "Of him are *ye in Christ* Jesus who of God is made unto us....righteousness."

Means of Justification. — Their necessity illustrated.

One more point deserves attention before we may close, the means of justification. To make their vast importance plain, permit me to introduce this simile. A message is to be sent by wire from New York to Chicago. Before this can be done, there must be at New York a battery, an instrument, and an operator to dispatch it, and at Chicago an instrument and an operator to receive it; also the connection by means of a wire must be made between the two terminal points. In other words, there must be a means for transmitting and a means for receiving the message. Manifestly these means contribute nothing whatever to the contents, value, or importance of the message: they do not make it, nor unmake it, nor improve it; they are simply the communicating medium; the message exists independent of them; yet, they are of the utmost importance; for without them the message is void and valueless, unavailable for the purposes of the originator.

In a similar manner, (only far exalted above this human mode of communication between far distances,) God has a means to transmit to men the message of His grace, the proclamation of the free pardon which He extends to every sinner, the glad tidings of justification. And He also supplies man with a means for receiving his gracious message.

MEANS OF TRANSFER ON THE PART OF GOD.

The means employed by God in transmitting to man the news of his salvation, hence also of his justification which is included in his salvation, are mentioned by Paul; "How shall they believe in him of whom they have not heard? And how shall they hear without a preacher?" (Rom. 10:14.) Again: "I declare unto you the gospel .... by which also ye are saved." (1. Cor. 15:1,2.) These two passages introduce the Word of God, as it is written, read, spoken, preached, as the saving means. Furthermore, we read: "He saved us by the washing of regeneration and renewing of the Holy Ghost." (Tit. 3: 5.) These words introduce what is called the visible Word, the holy sacraments, as a means of salvation. In reality, this second means does not differ from the first, for the holy sacraments, Baptism and the Lord's Supper, are made a life-bestowing, grace-bringing, justifying, and saving medium only through the accession of the Word of God, which, as our Church confesses, "is the chief thing in the Sacrament;" for, in Baptism "it is not the water indeed that does these great things, but the Word of God which is in and with the water;" and in the Lord's Supper, "it is not the eating and drinking, indeed, that does them, but the words here written, 'Given, and shed for you for the remission of sins.'" Accordingly, we hold that the means of justification, on the part of God, are the Word and the Sacraments.

In full accord with this our Church confesses: "Therefore their assertion is frivolous, when they say, 'That the body and blood of Christ are not given and shed for us in the Eucharist, and that for this reason we cannot obtain the forgiveness of sins in the sacrament of the Lord's Supper.' For, although this work was accomplished on the Cross, and the remission of sins obtained, yet they *cannot be communicated to us otherwise than through the word;* for how could we otherwise know that these things had been accomplished, or that they are presented to us, if they are not handed down to us through the Word? From what source do they know it, or how can they apprehend the remission of sins, and apply it to themselves, if they do not support themselves by, and believe in the Scripture and the Gospel? Now indeed the whole Gospel, and the article of the Creed, — I believe in a holy Christian church, forgiveness of sins, etc., — by virtue of the word, are embraced in this sacrament, and presented to us. Why then should we permit this treasure to be torn away from this sacrament, when at the same time they must acknowledge, that even these words are those which we hear every where in the Gospel? — And in truth, as little can they affirm that these words in the Sacrament are of no benefit, as they dare to affirm that the whole Gospel or the Word of God, apart from the sacrament is of no benefit." (Larg. Cat. P. V. p. 534.5.) "It would be impossible for a saint, however great and exalted, to endure the accusations of the divine law, the great power of Satan, the terrors of death, and finally, the despair and fear of hell, without *seizing hold of the divine promises*, the Gospel, as of a tree or branch in the great flood, in the strong, violent stream, among the waves, the surges, and pangs of death; or without *holding* by faith *to the word which proclaims grace*, and thus obtaining eternal life without any works, without the law, by grace alone." (Apol. III, 209.) "We should and must, therefore, constantly maintain that God will not confer with us frail beings, unless through his external word and sacraments. But all that is boasted of, independent of such word and sacraments, in reference to the Spirit, is criminal;" (German: "Das ist der Teufel.") (Smal. Art. VIII, p. 387.) "Therefore no one should boast of his works, because no one is justified by his own deeds; but he that is *just*, is *made so in baptism*, in Christ, since he became justified." (Apol. II, 177.) Last not least, the Augsburg Confession says: "These blessings" (eternal righseousness, the Holy Spirit, and eternal life,) *cannot be obtained otherwise than by the office of the ministry*, and by the administration of the holy sacraments. As St. Paul says, Rom. 1:16: "The gospel is the power of God unto salvation to every one that believeth." (Act. XXVII, p. 134.)

The view which our Church takes of the means by which God confers justification is this: The communication between God and the sinner, between heaven and earth, was established when God spoke to our fathers orally, when he sent them

preachers of righteousness, when the Holy Spirit inspired the
writers of old with the words of our Bible, when the Son of
God descended from his throne of glory to teach sinners the
way of salvation, when He instituted Baptism and Holy Com-
munion, when He founded the office of the gospel ministry.
Then it was that the connection was made, and the wires were
stretched across which the messages of peace and pardon have
been flashed by the power of Almighty God. The heavenly
battery of grace is at work now; do you hear the clicking of
the instrument? Go to church, and hear the servant of Christ
plead with fallen man, behold a child receiving baptism, observe
the communicants gather about the Table of the Lord; go into
your chamber and read your bible, let some good friend visit
you when you are in distress, or abed sick or dying, let him
cheer your faint heart with the everlasting comfort of the Word,
— and, my friend, you will be convinced that this means which
God employs is, indeed, capable of doing the work which God
has appointed for it, (comp. Isa. 55: 11.) that it is not a vain
display, not a senseless ceremony, not an empty emblem, but
that it is fraught with greater power than the wire which you
see trembling from the electrical charge, and flashing momentous
messages across oceans and continents.

But, here comes Dame Reason, throws up her nose, and
says: Pshaw! What is there in a handful of water, in a morsel
of bread, in a sip of wine, in your homely sermon and plain
preacher, in a catechism, in your little parochial school? What
good *can* they do? And having delivered herself of this great
wisdom, the good lady looks around for applause and approval,
imagining that she has said a wondrously smart thing. Very
well! We shall grant that a handful of water is, indeed, a handful of water, for that matter, and that an ox with his big eyes
will *see* just about as much efficacy in Holy Baptism, as Dame
Reason, with her little knowing eyes, so far as *seeing* plays a
figure in this matter. Yea, between Dame Reason and the
dumb brute the prophet would give the preference to the brute;
for, he says: "The ox knoweth his owner, and the ass his mas-
ter's crib: but Israel doth not know, my people doth not consider." (Isa. 1: 3.) However, let us reverse the argument: I
will stand near yonder railroad-track and say: What is there in
this pole, and in this piece of wire, and glass cap, can do much?
Presently the train comes puffing along, and I begin to argue:
Nothing but big pieces of cast iron, dead boards, ugly black

coal and steaming water — surely no meaning can possibly be attached to such an unsightly contrivance, there can be no power inherent in it, because there is nothing to indicate it! And thus arguing I should, indeed, claim to have said as smart a thing as human reason ever did say about the efficacy of the means of grace.

There is, then, this difference: when God's Word connects itself with any means, be it never so unseemly, that means becomes a power to accomplish the great things of God. True, these means do not work by their inherent natural power, but by communicated heavenly power. They are not merely exhibitions of something going on, but they have conferring, appropiating, sealing power. When God speaks, He acts; when He utters a word, He operates; His every syllable is a gift. He is, indeed, the doer, but He does what He does by these means.

To these means He has bound and restricted us. There is where we shall seek and find our salvation. Unless we find it there, we shall forever remain without it. Neglect of the means of grace, therefore, is the greatest harm which a person can inflict upon himself. Hence, we should be eager to make the most diligent use of them, and thus obtain and seal to ourselves the message of peace which the Lord sends.

MEANS FOR MAN'S ACCEPTANCE.

This message must be received by the sinner who is dead, who, in spiritual matters, represents a lifeless corpse. What is the means by which this is effected? "The righteousness of God," says St. Paul, "is by faith of Jesus Christ unto all and upon all them that believe." (Rom. 3:22.) The righteousness of God is unto and upon all, i. e. it extends to them and they obtain it by a wonderful instrument of God's workmanship and God's giving, — faith. *Faith,* as is evident from the language of this text, *deals with the transfer of the righteousness of God to man;* it is the receiving hand by which the proffered gifts of God are grasped. — However, we must note that the apostle in this text mentions also the object of faith "Jesus Christ." By faith in Jesus Christ the righteousness of God is unto and upon all them that believe. In like manner he speaks of faith as the justifying means in the next chapter when he introduces the example of believing Abraham, whom he calls "the father of them that believe;" (v. 11.) vv. 23–25 he writes: "Now it was not written for his sake alone, that it was imputed to him; but for us also, to whom it shall be imputed if we *believe in him that raised up Jesus* our Lord from the dead; who was delivered for our offences, and was raised again for our justification." And again, in Gal. 2: 20 the same apostle describes the life which he was then living thus: "The life which I now live in the flesh, I live *by the faith of the Son of God, who loved me and gave himself for me.*"

It is not without purpose that the Scriptures, in speaking of justifying faith, mention in close connection with it the work of Our Savior. By this close connection the relation of faith to justification is to be made quite plain: we are, by no means, to imagine that our justification is effected on account of, or in view of our faith, but justification is on account of the Lord who gave Himself for us; it is made ours, however, by faith. Faith is here viewed not as an act of merit, even of the least significance, but only as the means, mode, and manner of appropriation. Accordingly, the Form of Concord states: "Faith justifies us not because it is a work of great value and an eminent virtue but because it apprehends and receives the merit of Christ in the promise of the holy gospel; for this merit must be applied and appropriated unto ourselves through faith, if we shall be justified by *it.*" (III, 631.) And the Augsburg Confession teaches that "forgiveness of sin," i. e. justification "is obtained by true repentance, which consists in contrition and besides, in faith in the gospel or absolution — namely that sins are forgiven and grace is obtained through Christ." (——p. 112.)

FAITH AND WORKS.

These observations will unerringly direct us to view and speak aright of faith in its relation to the dealings of God with sinful man, hence also to justification; a matter which is of special importance to the Lutheran Church of our time and place. The Form of Concord instructs us that to a correct presentation of the doctrine of justification belongs emphatic mention of the so-called "particulae exclusivae." It says: "We believe, teach, and confess that for the preservation of the true doctrine concerning the righteousness of faith before God, the particulae exclusivae, that is, the following words of the holy apostle Paul, by which the merit of Christ is wholly separated from our works, and the honor attributed to Christ alone, are to be maintained with special diligence, as when the holy apostle

Paul writes, "by grace," Eph. 2: 5, 8: "freely," Rom. 3: 24; "without the law," Rom. 3: 21; Gal. 3: 11; "without works," Rom. 4: 6; "without the deeds of the law," Rom. 3: 28; all of which words signify alike that we are righteous and saved through faith in Christ alone." (Epit. III, 561.2.)

Accordingly, two things in the gracious economy of God must forever remain as widely separated as heaven and earth, as day and night; these two things are: *faith and works.* Whatever is of faith is not of works, and a dealer in works holds no stock in the bank of faith. The case really stands thus: He that believeth, i. e. worketh not, is saved. Works are by the law, faith is by the gospel; works are the children of Moses, faith that of Christ; work-mongers are Ishmaelites, begotten of the bondwoman Hagar, and representing the natural strength of their father; the followers of faith are Isaacs, begotten of Sarah, the freewoman, and representing the power of God who is faithful in what He promises. These two cannot abide in the same estate, nor can the estate be divided between them. Ishmael will scorn Isaac and merit ejection from the manor; Isaac must be heir alone.

"IN VIEW OF FAITH."

It is evident, then, that to represent *faith as that work which* MAN *must perform*, in order to be saved, is a clean departure from biblical theology, and because such a departure entails the most disastrous consequences, it is the rankest heresy in Christendom; for, it virtually destroys the main distinctive doctrine of Christianity, and practically paganizes the Church of Christ. So soon as faith is classified under the general head of works which man must perform, so long as faith, and that which leads to faith, is brought in to explain the difference between men in conversion and justification, we have become Jews, Turks, and heathen. The only difference is: their works are avowedly legalistic; ours should be such no less, did we not manage to put some gospel-gloss over it, by pretending that this faith is of God's operation. However, that does not make a particle of difference, so long as it is maintained that faith is a condition which man must fulfill in order to be saved.

But, it is being argued that man must perform the act of believing, that it would be absurd to imagine that God would believe for him; consequently, faith must be, in part at least, man's work. Indeed, man must be the believer; that is true. So man must also drink the water that slacks *his* thirst, no one can drink it for him; man must eat the bread that stills *his* hunger, no one can eat it for him; man must himself sleep, in order to be rested, no one can sleep for him. Such is the order which the Lord has ordained both in the economy of His power and in that of His grace. Actually these matters are most trivial truisms which only simpletons would deny. But, the question is not at all: *Who* must believe? but, whether believing is doing something. When our adversaries draw this destructive inference: Consequently, man has something to do with his salvation, yea, when a professor of theology who certainly *could* know better, informs us that, "rightly understood" (!!) man's work is of decisive moment, we emphatically enter our protest. We have been taught thus by Scripture: Because man *can*NOT perform any works which have a favorable bearing on his salvation, hence also on his justification, THEREFORE *he must believe;* faith should not be required, were man capable of performing works.

FAITH CONSISTS IN RECEIVING.

After all, *what is faith?* The Scriptures speak of *faith* as *an accepting.* So Paul; "As ye have therefore *received* Christ Jesus the Lord, so walk ye in him." (Col. 2: 6.) So John, who even goes a step further in that he uses believing in Christ and accepting Christ indiscriminately; "But as many as *received* him to them he gave power to become the sons of God, even to them that *believe* on his name. (John 1: 12.) And in his last priestly prayer he makes this statement; "I have given unto them the words which thou gavest me, and they have *received* them, and I have known surely that I came out from thee, and they have *believed* that thou didst send me." (John 17: 8.) On the other hand, *not believing* in Christ is *not receiving* Him. "He came unto his own, and his own received him not." (John 1: 11.) Faith, therefore, is the means for accepting Christ. As an armless person cannot take anything, as where there is no vessel nothing can be poured out to one, so where there is no faith, no salvation is possible, as there is nothing to receive and hold it in. For this reason the Holy Spirit in quite a number of places teaches that we are justified *by* or *through* faith, but *nowhere* does He teach that we are justified *on account of*, in *consideration of*, or *in view of faith.*

Is Faith prior to justification?

Still, is not faith, in point of time, prior to justification? Is not this a true conception of the relation of faith to justification, viz. faith precedes, justification follows, granting that these two acts are not separated the one from the other by a longer interval of time than, let us say, one second? Even this view will be found to be erroneous.

We cannot scripturally assume a state in which man, although possessing faith, is still not justified. To conceive the possibility of an unjustified believer, even for one second, is as gross an anomaly as to conceive of a sour lump sugar, of dry water, or of a calm cyclone. Logicians call such terms "contradictio in adjecto," i. e., a case in which the qualifying word which is added to another word for the purpose of determining its meaning more fully, instead of determining it, contradicts it. Sour sugar is simply no sugar; dry water no water; a calm cyclone no cyclone; in like manner, a faith that does not justify is worthless. Faith is the justifying means all the time, even at its very first beginning; even a little spark of faith justifies; for the Lord "will not quench the smoking flax," (Isa. 42: 3) and the Form of Concord says: 'For whosoever believeth in the Son of God, *be it with a weak or strong faith*, hath everlasting life. This worthiness consists, not in a greater or a less weakness or strength of faith, but in the merits of Christ, in which the sorrowing father, who was weak in faith, and who is mentioned in the 9th. ch. and 24th. verse of Mark, shared, as well as Abraham, Paul and others, who had a joyful and a strong faith." (Decl. VII. p. 675.) It is a mere figment of human reason to maintain that in its very first stage faith has not yet justifying power. Now, a person either has or has not faith. Accordingly, we hold that a believer is justified from the moment when he believes, and that his faith and his justification coincide in time.

The Form of Concord says: "*Faith* is imputed to us *for righteousness*." (Epit. III, p. 561.) Again: "The righteousness of faith is the remission of sins, reconciliation with God, and our adoption as children of God, for the sake of the obedience of Christ alone, which *obedience* is imputed *for righteousness*, through faith only, by grace alone, unto all true believers; and thus in consequence of it, they are absolved from all their unrighteousness." (Decl. III, 629. 30.) Comparing these two statements we find that our Confessions state, now that faith, now that the obedience of Christ is imputed to us for righteousness; now it is faith that justifies, now the work of the Redeemer, How are we to understand this? If these terms, faith and the obedience of Christ, can be used inter-changeably or, as it were, indiscriminately, when that which justifies is being set forth, surely there must be a certain similitude or equality or close connection between them. The connection exists; justifying faith can never be considered apart from the obedience of Christ. Faith is the hand, the obedience of Christ the jewel which this hand grasps; faith is the vessel, the merits of Christ the water of life which is caught in this vessel; faith is the shell, the work of Christ is the sweet kernel. True, the hand, the vessel, the shell are needed requisites, yet their efficacy is owing, not to what they *are*, but to what they *contain*.

Here lies one of the great errors of men who, like the Ohio Synod, teach the doctrine "in view of faith." Faith is by them viewed as a virtue, not as a mere means. When we speak of the justifying power of faith we do *not* mean to *ascribe that power to the act of man's believing*, performed by him through the grace of God, but THE POWER ATTACHES ONLY AND SOLELY TO THAT WHICH THIS FAITH GRASPS. Were it not for the inestimable merits of Our Blessed Redeemer the most fervent and heroic faith of men would be in vain. Justifying faith cannot be considered otherwise than in the very closest connection with the work of Christ.

Faith, therefore, cannot be first else justification would necessarily be on account of faith. Nor can justification be first, else it should be without faith ; these two are contemporaneous. Believing we are justified: being justified we believe.

Lord Jesus, Thou who receivest sinners, we believe that Thou art our sole Redeemer, and that the glory of our righteousness belongs entirely to Thee. Help Thou our unbelief and preserve us in the faith of the gospel of free grace. O Christ Thou Lamb of God, that takest away the sins of the world, have mercy on us and grant us Thy peace. Amen.